THE
EVERYBODY
CLUB

Linda Hayen

Nancy Loewen & Linda Hayen

Illustrated by Yana Zybina

For Carissa

Are you **big**?

Are you small?

Are you **LOUD?**

Are you shy?

Do you smile?

Do you dream?

Do you laugh?

Do you try?

Then follow me!
Right this way.

The Everybody Club
needs YOU today!

Here's your badge.
Come on, let's go.
We've lots to do
and a CLUB to grow!

**Did you make
a mistake?**

**Did you drop
the ball?**

Don't you worry! No harm done.

The Everybody Club NEEDS members like you:

Are you sad sometimes?

Are you scared you'll fall?

That's just life — for EVERYONE!

BRAVE and STRONG and TOUGH and TRUE.

So many people!
They're members too.
They belong,
like me and you.
Tell them all:
You're a member.
It's official.

The
Everybody Club
is **BENEFICIAL!**

Wish Plan Snip Clip

Shake - Shake WHIRL!

Paint

Pound

Blow

Show

Jump

Flip

TWIRL!

Spread the word!

Whisper it

Shake on it

Send it in a note

Sing it

SHOUT IT

Put it on a...

EVERYBODY

...FLOAT!

A parade of EVERYBODIES!
A JOLLY JAMBOREE!

The **EVERYBODY CLUB**
turns **THEY** to **WE**.

My daughter, Carissa, was an intelligent girl with a huge heart. Her brother, Phillip, 20 months younger, was born with cerebral palsy; he was unable to walk or talk. Another brother, Todd, was six years younger, and he and Carissa played together often.

One day when Carissa was about nine years old, she started the Everybody Club. She was President and Todd and Phillip were Members, along with all her stuffed animals and all her dolls. She made membership cards and badges and wrote out "rules" —but the only real purpose of the club was so that everybody could belong.

Carissa never lost that sense of inclusion and community. As a teenager, she was the one friends would come to whenever they were having conflicts. She was the one who would thoughtfully try to solve problems, both in her immediate world and in society. As a sophomore in high school, she went on a school trip to Washington, D.C., and decided she wanted to become a politician to try to help nations get along with one another.

Shortly after the D.C. trip, in May of 2000, Carissa died in a car accident.

So many years have passed, but I still often find myself viewing the world through her eyes. I know she would have been dismayed and heartbroken about the injustices that we see around us every day— racism, gun violence, economic disparity, and so many others. And she would have committed herself to making things better.

This book is dedicated to Carissa and her ideals.
Let's all have a club that includes EVERYBODY.

– Linda Hayen

Everybody
Club

EC

EVERYBODY
CLUB

these

you can do anything!
Love carissa

make

other

happy

Nancy Loewen

Nancy Loewen grew up on a farm in southwestern Minnesota, surrounded by library books and cats. She's published more than 140 books for children. *Four to the Pole* (co-authored with polar explorer Ann Bancroft) and *The LAST Day of Kindergarten* were Minnesota Book Award finalists. Her Writer's Toolbox series received a Distinguished Achievement Award from the Association of Educational Publishers. Nancy lives in Saint Paul and has an MFA in Creative Writing from Hamline University. She has two young adult children and a cat who sometimes bites her knees under the table as she writes.

Linda Hayen

Linda Hayen loves stories and plays and connecting with people. She has an MS in Community Health Education from the University of Illinois and worked with seniors in the healthcare field for many years. Her other passion is community theater, and you may see her onstage or behind the scenes at various locations around the Twin Cities. She has led and participated in numerous support groups and believes strongly in including everyone, always. Her two living children, Phillip and Todd, are proud members of The Everybody Club. This is her first experience in collaborating on a children's book, and it has been wonderful in every way.

Yana Zybina

Yana Zybina is an illustrator from southwestern Russia. She has always loved to draw. Originally a designer, she was inspired to become an illustrator when her son was born and she found herself painting pictures of him in all his daily activities. Yana creates her pictures traditionally, using paper and watercolors; her titles include *Mommy Goes to Yoga* and *The Quarantine Kid*. She hopes that her illustrations will help kids understand the world around them—and make them smile.

Heather Homa designer
Heather Homa is an artist living in Minneapolis. She immerses herself equally in design, illustration, gardening, and roasting marshmallows.

PHOTOS (FROM TOP TO BOTTOM): MICHAEL PANKRATZ, ANNA KHODYREVA, KAREN HOMA

Made in the USA
Monee, IL
21 March 2021